MY BIKE

D O N N A   J A K O B

ILLUSTRATED BY NELLE DAVIS

HYPERION BOOKS FOR CHILDREN / NEW YORK

my bike.

Yesterday

I could stand by the curb
and push off...sort of.

Today I soar down the street.

Yesterday the pedals
kept getting stuck
on their way up
to my feet.

Today the pedals go 'round and 'round
with my feet in perfect rhythm.

Yesterday the front wheel wobbled
from left to right,
even with my dad holding me.

Today the wheels glide smoothly straight ahead on the dark pavement.

Yesterday
I fell a lot
in a tangled heap.

Today I ride with the wind in my face.

Yesterday I said I liked scooters best.

Today
I gave my scooter
to my little sister.

Yesterday,
from my front stoop,
I watched all the bike riders.

Yesterday
I thought today
would never come.

Today I learned to *ride*

my bike.

For Zachary, my son,
who does indeed ride
with the wind in his face,
for Stephen, my husband,
who believed yesterday
that today would come,
and for Howard, my editor.
—D.J.

For Ben and for my family.
—N.D.

Text © 1994 by Donna Jakob. Illustrations © 1994 by Nelle Davis.
All rights reserved.
Printed in Singapore.
For information address Hyperion Books for Children,
114 Fifth Avenue, New York, New York 10011.
FIRST EDITION
1 3 5 7 9 10 8 6 4 2

Library of Congress Cataloging-in-Publication Data
Jakob, Donna.
My bike/Donna Jakob; illustrated by Nelle Davis.
p. cm.
Summary: A boy learns the difference between yesterday when he
could not ride his bike and today when he leads all the bicyclists.
ISBN 1-56282-454-6 (trade)—ISBN 1-56282-455-4 (lib. bdg.)
[1. Bicycles and bicycling—Fiction.] I. Davis, Nelle, ill.
II. Title
PZ7. J153554My 1994
[E]—dc20   93-5788   CIP   AC

The artwork for each picture is prepared
using scratchboard, watercolor, marker, and film.
This book is set in 24-point Ronda.

DATE			